World Heritage

Carmel Reilly

First published in 2007 by Cengage Learning Australia
www.cengage.com.au

This edition published in 2008 under the imprint of Nelson Thornes Ltd,
Delta Place, 27 Bath Road, Cheltenham, United Kingdom, GL53 7TH

10 9 8 7 6 5 4 3 2
11 10 09 08

Text © 2007 Cengage Learning Australia Pty Ltd ABN 14058280149
(incorporated in Victoria)

The right of Carmel Reilly to be identified as author of this work has been asserted by him/her
in accordance with the Copyright, Designs and Patents Act 1988

All rights reserved. No part of this publication may be reproduced or transmitted in any form or
by any means, electronic or mechanical, including photocopy, recording or any information storage
and retrieval system, without permission in writing from the publisher or under licence from the
Copyright Licensing Agency Limited, of 90 Tottenham Court Road, London W1T 4LP.

Any person who commits any unauthorised act in relation to this publication may be
liable to criminal prosecution and civil claims for damages.

World Heritage
ISBN 978-1-4085-0139-9

Text by Carmel Reilly
Edited by Bec Quinn
Designed by James Lowe
Series Design by James Lowe
Production Controller Seona Galbally
Photo Research by Corrina Tauschke
Audio recordings by Juliet Hill, Picture Start
Spoken by Matthew King and Abbe Holmes
Printed in China by 1010 Printing International Ltd

Website www.nelsonthornes.com

Acknowledgements
The author and publisher would like to acknowledge permission to reproduce material from
the following sources:
Photographs by Corbis/Darrell Gulin, p. 13 bottom; Corbis/Frans Lanting, p. 15 top; Corbis/Free Agents Limited/
Dallas and John Heaton, p. 23 top; Corbis/Horacio Villalobos, p. 4 inset; Corbis/Jonathan Blair, pp. 18 bottom, 19;
Corbis/Jose Fuste Raga, p. 11; Corbis/Lloyd Cuff, p. 10; Corbis/Otto Lang, p. 13 top; Corbis/Paul Almasy, p. 9 inset;
Corbis/Robert Harding World Imagery, pp. 9, 15 bottom, 22; Corbis/Robert Harding World Imagery/Christian
Kober, p. 14 top; Corbis/Roger Wood, p. 12; Corbis/Stuart Westmorland, p. 21 bottom; Corbis/Superstock Inc.,
p. 20; Corbis/Wolfgang Kaehler, p. 18 top; Getty Images/J/Photodisc Green/John Wang, p. 7; Getty Images/National
Geographic/Nicole Duplaix, p. 17 top; Getty Images/Photographer's Choice/Fotoworld, p. 6 top; Getty Images/
Photographer's Choice/Glen Allison, p. 6 bottom; Getty Images/The Bridgeman Art Library, p. 17 bottom; Lonely
Planet Images/Chris Bell, p. 14 inset; Lonely Planet Images/Greg Elms, p. 23 bottom; Lonely Planet Images/Jane
Sweeney, p. 8 top; Lonely Planet Images/John Hay, p. 16; Lonely Planet Images/Krzysztof Dydynski, p. 23 inset;
Lonely Planet Images/Leonard Douglas Zell, p. 21 top; Lonely Planet Images/Paul Greenway, p. 8 bottom; Lonely
Planet Images/Richard I'Anson, pp. front cover, 3, 5, 5 inset; Masterfile/Ed Gifford, back cover; Photolibrary/
Airphoto Australia/Peter Harrison, p. 4; Photolibrary/Robert Harding Picture Library Ltd/Sylvain Grandadam, p. 14
bottom; Photolibrary/The Travel Library Limited, p. 15 inset.

World Heritage

Carmel Reilly

Contents

Chapter 1	**The World Heritage List**	4
Chapter 2	**Sites in Danger**	8
Chapter 3	**How the World Heritage List Began**	10
Chapter 4	**Venice**	16
Chapter 5	**The Great Barrier Reef**	20
Chapter 6	**How the World Heritage List Helps**	22
Glossary and Index		24

Chapter 1
THE WORLD HERITAGE LIST

The World Heritage List was set up in 1972, by the United Nations Educational, Scientific and Cultural Organization (UNESCO). It was set up to save and care for special places around the world.

Some places on the World Heritage List are natural **sites**, like Australia's Great Barrier Reef.
Other places on the list are cultural sites, like Venice in Italy.
Cultural sites have been made by people, and include buildings and cities.

the Great Barrier Reef

Jim Jim Falls, Kakadu National Park

Aboriginal rock art, Kakadu National Park

Some places on the list are both natural and cultural sites, like Kakadu National Park in Australia. These places are important for both natural and cultural reasons.

Heritage is about things from the past.
Things that are part of our heritage can be passed from one **generation** to another,
and they are important for the future.

Catherine's Palace, St Petersburg, Russia

a temple at Angkor Wat, Cambodia

the Great Wall of China

Places that are sites on the World Heritage List
are of great interest and value.
Many of them are also in danger.
These places need to be looked after
so they will be here
for future generations to enjoy.

Chapter 2
SITES IN DANGER

Many world heritage sites are in danger of being lost or damaged because of **environmental** changes. These changes include **global warming** and pollution.

The Perito Moreno glacier, in Argentina, is in danger because of global warming.

The old city of Bam, in Iran, has been damaged by earthquakes.

a buddha at Bamiyan, Afghanistan

The cultural heritage of the buddhas at Bamiyan has been damaged by war.

Other world heritage sites are in danger of being lost or damaged because of our way of life.

Today, some countries are at war, and in a lot of other countries, there isn't enough money to fix these special places or keep them safe.

Chapter 3
HOW THE WORLD HERITAGE LIST BEGAN

In the 1950s, the Egyptian government decided to build a dam in the Aswan Valley to make electric power.

the Aswan Dam on the Nile River

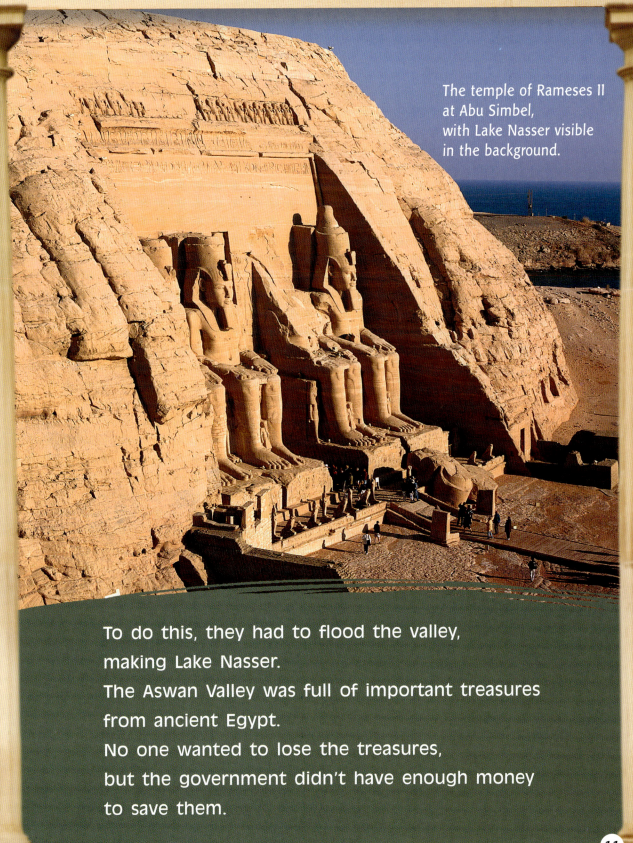

The temple of Rameses II at Abu Simbel, with Lake Nasser visible in the background.

To do this, they had to flood the valley, making Lake Nasser.
The Aswan Valley was full of important treasures from ancient Egypt.
No one wanted to lose the treasures, but the government didn't have enough money to save them.

UNESCO looked into Egypt's problem and decided to ask other countries to help.

A sphinx, relocated to the Nile River when the dam was built.

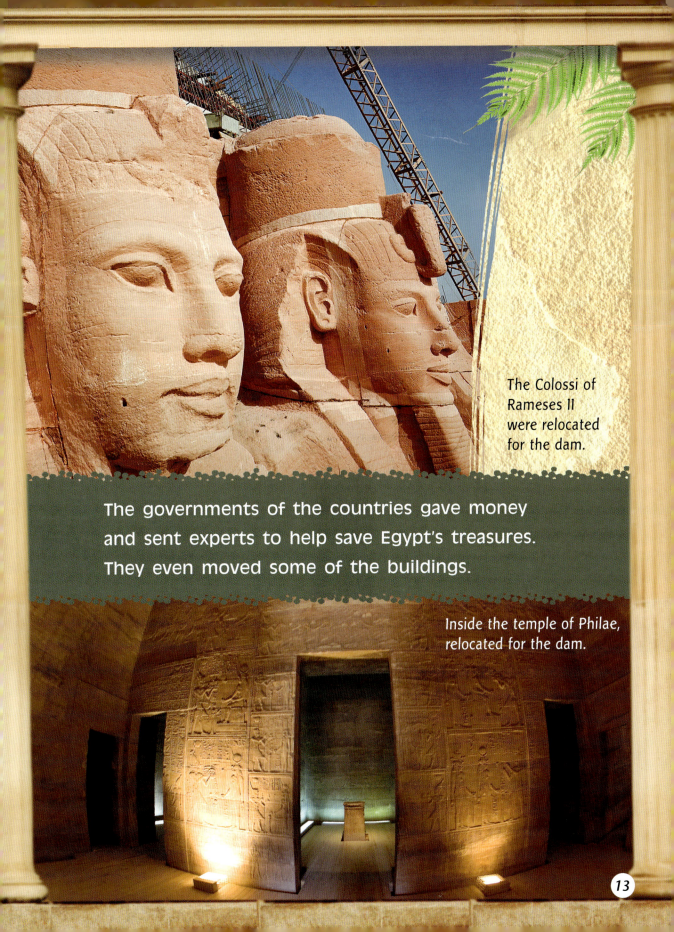

The Colossi of Rameses II were relocated for the dam.

The governments of the countries gave money and sent experts to help save Egypt's treasures. They even moved some of the buildings.

Inside the temple of Philae, relocated for the dam.

UNESCO then realised that it was possible to save other sites that might also be in danger.

the Ryoan-ji Temple dry stone garden, Japan

King penguins, Macquarie Island

Tourists taking photos of Iguanas in the Galapagos Islands.

ruins at Machu Picchu, Peru

the Makli hill tombs, Pakistan

Notre Dame Cathedral, Paris

In 1972, UNESCO set up the World Heritage List to name the places it believed were the most important. Today, there are more than 830 sites in 137 countries on the World Heritage List.

VENICE

Venice is a very old city in Italy.
It was put on the World Heritage List in 1987.

The city was built hundreds of years ago,
on islands near the coast.
Instead of roads, it has waterways.
There are no cars,
and people travel around by boat.

Venice is also full of old and beautiful works of art and buildings that cannot be found anywhere else in the world.

the lion of St Mark

Venice's islands are slowly sinking, and its art and buildings are in danger of being lost.

floodwaters in St Mark's Square

Venice's islands have been slowly sinking for a long time, but they are sinking much faster now because of global warming and rising sea levels.

Because Venice is on the World Heritage List, expert help and money are given to the city to help protect it.

people walking above the floodwaters in St Mark's Square

Chapter 5

THE GREAT BARRIER REEF

The Great Barrier Reef was included on the World Heritage List in 1981.
Like Venice, the reef is in danger because of global warming.
Scientists believe that plants and animals living on the reef will die if the sea gets too hot.

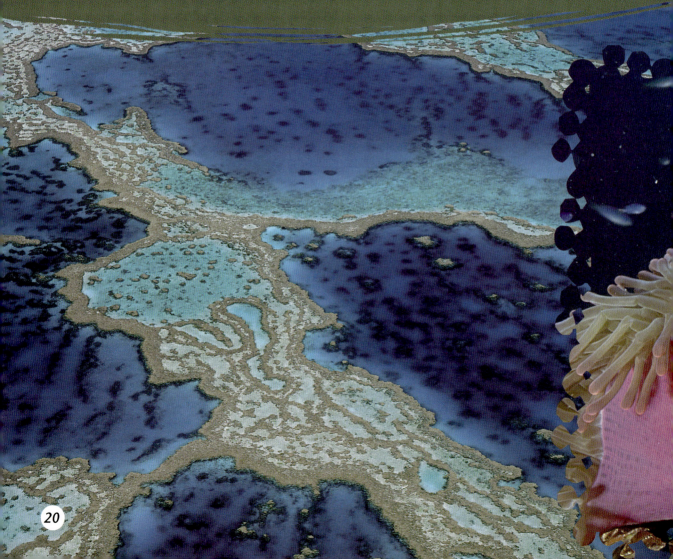

a scientist monitoring the reef

People have always known how special the Great Barrier Reef is.
But, because it's on the World Heritage List, people are now helping to protect it.

Chapter 6
HOW THE WORLD HERITAGE LIST HELPS

Being on the World Heritage List helps sites in danger by:

- making people everywhere see how important a site is to world heritage

- showing people how changes to the environment, and other problems, can damage both natural and cultural sites

- providing more money and expert help from UNESCO to care for and look after the sites.

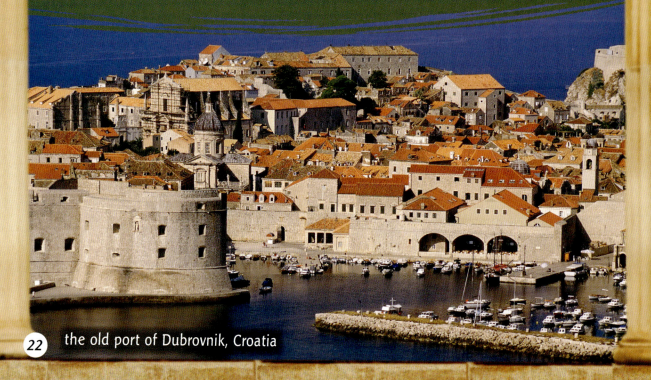

the old port of Dubrovnik, Croatia

pyramids at Giza, Egypt

flamingoes at Lake Ngorongoro, Tanzania

Wieliczka salt mine, Poland

Glossary

environmental   relating to the physical surroundings of an area

generation   all the people born at about the same time

global warming   the increase in temperature of the Earth's atmosphere, caused by the greenhouse effect

heritage   a nation's historic buildings and countryside

sites   the land or ground where buildings, cities or natural formations are located

Index

Aswan Valley   10–11

Egypt   11, 12–13

global warming   8, 19, 20

Great Barrier Reef   4, 20–21

heritage   6

Kakadu National Park   5

UNESCO   4, 12, 14–15, 22

Venice   4, 16–19

World Heritage List   4, 7, 15, 16, 19, 20–21, 22